TOXIC

" Four huge men in silver-coloured, ancient Roman armour – helmets, tunics and iron breastplates – were looming over them, spears raised in the air.

'I guess your little journey has just ended,' said one of the soldiers.

He and the other soldiers raised their spears to strike. "

GLADIATOR
REVIVAL

Gladiator Revival
by Jonny Zucker
Illustrated by Alan Brown

Published by Ransom Publishing Ltd.
Radley House, 8 St. Cross Road, Winchester, Hampshire
SO23 9HX, UK
www.ransom.co.uk

ISBN   978 178127 712 6
First published in 2015

GLADIATOR
REVIVAL

JONNY ZUCKER

ILLUSTRATED BY
ALAN BROWN

Ransom

Chapter 1

THWACK!

A metal-tipped spear shot down the tunnel a centimetre above Nick and Kat's head.

'WHAT'S GOING ON?' shouted Kat in panic.

'I DON'T KNOW!' replied Nick. 'BUT RUN!'

*****

Ten minutes ago, Nick and Kat Ellis had been staring up at Rome's giant Coliseum. They were on holiday and they'd split from their parents for a few hours.

Nick had spotted a tattered door on the other side of the road and he'd insisted they open it and explore.

He was a boy who loved adventure.

The door had led to this dimly lit, downward-sloping tunnel.

They'd only gone a few paces when the spear had been launched at them.

*****

THWACK!

There was another one, bouncing off the tunnel wall with a horrible clanging echo.

In horror, they upped their speed, terrified of being hit.

'LOOK! UP AHEAD!' shouted Nick.

They could see a circle of light at the end of the tunnel. Sprinting towards it, they ran into what looked exactly like an ancient Roman market.

People in old Roman clothes were selling fruit, vegetables and coloured spices. Strange gold coins were being passed between customers and stallholders.

'THIS WAY!' barked Nick, leaping out of the way of another flying spear.

They raced between some squawking chickens and leapt over a pile of logs.

They'd just run through an archway at the far end of the market when they were suddenly surrounded.

Four huge men in silver-coloured, ancient Roman armour – helmets, tunics and iron breastplates – were looming over them, spears raised in the air.

'I guess your little journey has just ended,' said one of the soldiers.

He and the other soldiers raised their spears to strike.

CHAPTER 2

'STOP!' cried a loud voice.

Another soldier, this one in gold-coloured armour, strode towards them.

The four soldiers immediately lowered their spears, bowed their heads and stood to one side.

'I am Cassius, your trainer,' declared the gold-covered soldier, fixing his eyes on Nick and Kat. 'You are late.'

'Late for what?' asked Kat.

'Do not try and be clever with me,' replied Cassius, shooing the other soldiers away. 'There is much work to be done; we need to move right now.'

'Sorry,' said Nick, 'but is this a film set? Are you all actors?'

'Enough questions,' snapped Cassius. 'Just follow me.'

Nick and Kat looked at each other.

'If it's not a film, it could be some kind of theatre show,' Nick whispered. 'It might be fun.'

Kat sighed. 'It's got to be better than facing those four spear-guys again.'

Cassius was already some way ahead of them, so they hurried forward to catch him up.

'Is this a museum?' asked Kat. 'Because if it is, it's way better than the museums back home. They might have a few people dressed up, but nothing like this. It's really impressive.'

Cassius ignored her. He led them down several stone passageways, past an old man baking some kind of bread over an open fire and into a bright courtyard. Two women in brown and red tunics were hanging woollen shirts on a line to dry.

Cassius pulled open a barred black door. He shoved Nick and Kat inside a small, damp cell. Then he slammed the door shut.

'HEY!' shouted Kat. 'WHAT ARE YOU DOING?'

'Welcome to your new home,' said Cassius. He locked the door with a large key and strode off.

A few seconds later, he was gone from sight.

CHAPTER 3

The cell had a low ceiling and a cold stone floor. A cockroach scuttled into a hole.

'This is brilliant!' said Nick. 'Maybe it's a kids' TV show and we're going to be the stars!'

'What kind of rubbish TV programme has kids being locked up?' groaned Kat.

*****

It wasn't long before Cassius reappeared. He was carrying two small suits of shiny metal armour.

He unlocked the door and said gruffly, 'Put these on.'

Kat was about to protest, but Nick shook his head. 'Let's just go along with it,' he said.

They put the armour on over their clothes and then Cassius led them down several more passageways. He stopped when they came to a large yard covered in sand.

'We'll start with fitness,' he declared. 'Jog ten times round this yard.'

'Are you a PE teacher?' asked Nick.

'Just do it!' shouted Cassius.

They started running.

They were both good runners, so they found it easy.

'Not bad,' said Cassius.

Next he got them to do press-ups and sit-ups, then some more running.

'Remember,' he told them. 'Fitness alone will not be enough when you enter the Coliseum.'

'The Coliseum!' gasped Kat. 'Is that what this is all about? Are you a tour guide?'

'Stop talking nonsense!' said Cassius irritably. 'You both know that you are here to be trained as young gladiators, and that I am your teacher.'

'But it's just a game isn't it?' said Nick.

'A GAME?' thundered Cassius. 'THIS IS NOT A GAME!'

He stepped out of the yard and came back a few moments later, pushing a huge model of a gigantic, hideous-looking creature, covered in shiny, scaly green skin. It had red eyes, giant claws and sharp white fangs.

'This will be your enemy in the Coliseum,' Cassius informed them.

'Say hello to *The Beast*.'

Chapter 4

Nick burst out laughing.

'OK,' he said. 'Can we stop the acting now. We should be heading back to our parents and … '

Cassius thumped the side of the model with his fist.

'Do you want the beast to kill you, or do you want me to teach you how to fight it?' he demanded.

Nick frowned in confusion.

'We will now focus on how to jump and dive out of its way,' said Cassius. 'The first move is the sideways dive.'

He stood behind the model and pushed it rapidly towards them.

Nick dived right, Kat dived left. Both of them got whacked on the leg by the model.

'Not quick enough!' said Cassius.

They spent the next thirty minutes trying out all sorts of dives, leaps and jumps to avoid the big model beast.

'Now we are going to see how fast you can run,' said Cassius.

He stood behind the model and suddenly pushed it quickly towards them, roaring at the top of his voice.

Even though he was pushing the large model of the beast, Cassius could run surprisingly fast.

Nick and Kat were jolted in shock and pelted off in opposite directions. The beast hared after Nick, who only just managed to outrun it.

Then it bore down on Kat. She rushed to the far side of the yard as the model raced after her.

She jumped to her left and the beast banged into a wall.

'Now for combat,' announced Cassius, throwing a small shield and sword to each of them.

'Your job is to kill the beast before it kills you.'

Kat gulped.

For the next hour they practised smashing their shields through the air to repel the beast.

Then they had a go at tackling the beast with their swords.

'OK,' said Cassius finally. 'We're done.'

He brought the model to a halt.

'Er … Cassius,' said Nick. 'When are we going to fight this beast?'

Cassius gave them both a long hard look.

'Tonight,' he replied.

CHAPTER 5

'Tonight!' cried Kat. 'There is NO WAY I am going into the Coliseum to fight a beast. Not tonight and not on any other night!'

'I'm with Kat on this one,' said Nick. 'It's time for us to go.'

'You are going nowhere!' hissed Cassius, the veins bulging in his neck.

'Yes we are!' replied Nick. 'Come on Kat!'

He grabbed her by the elbow and they ran out of the yard.

'COME BACK HERE!' yelled Cassius.

'This way,' said Nick.

They turned right and sprinted back towards the courtyard where the cell was.

'STOP!' screamed Cassius.

Down passageways they ran, with Cassius hot on their heels.

They flew into the market and smashed into a fruit stall, sending a huge pile of pears crashing onto the ground.

'HEY!' shouted the stall-keeper furiously. He reached out to grab Nick and Kat, but slipped on the carpet of rolling fruit.

Kat barged into a barrel of wine that cracked open. Sweet-smelling red liquid poured onto the ground.

'Look! There's the tunnel we came down!' cried Nick.

They had just made it to the entrance when they heard a triumphant yell and firm hands grabbed them by their collars.

'GOT YOU!' hissed Cassius triumphantly.

Chapter 6

Nick and Kat kicked out their legs. They lashed out their arms. They screamed at the top of their voices.

But it was no good. Cassius was far stronger than them.

A few minutes later they reached the courtyard.

Cassius opened the cell door and chucked them inside, as if they were sacks of potatoes.

He locked the door and stormed off.

'Hang on,' said Nick, pulling his mobile phone out of his pocket. 'I should have thought of this before! Let's phone Mum and Dad.'

But the phone had no reception.

'Maybe the walls of this cell are too thick to get a mobile signal,' said Kat.

'Maybe we're in Roman times and they just haven't invented mobile phones yet,' answered Nick.

He looked at Kat, sighed, and put the phone away.

*****

A short while later, it started getting dark outside.

'This is bizarre,' said Kat. 'They seem to have their own micro-climate down here.'

'Do you really think we'll have to fight a beast inside the Coliseum?' asked Nick anxiously.

'I don't know,' said Kat, biting her bottom lip.

*****

Before long Cassius turned up again.

'I have good news,' he informed them.

'What is it?' asked Kat.

'I have told the city's leaders that you two are not ready to take on the beast. They have agreed to set you free.'

'That's brilliant,' cried Nick, jumping to his feet and pulling Kat up with him.

'You can return home,' said Cassius, unlocking the cell door.

'Thanks so much,' beamed Kat, relief all over her face. 'We'll head back up that tunnel. Please could you keep those spear-throwing soldiers away from us?'

Cassius nodded and led them along a series of twisting paths. They walked past a stonemason chipping away at a giant block of granite and strode across a slatted wooden bridge stretching over a stream.

They heard a noise in the distance, and as they walked it got louder. Soon they could hear it was the sound of a giant crowd.

They turned a corner and there, looming above them, was a massive stone structure with large flags on the ramparts, swaying in the breeze.

'That is the Coliseum,' said Cassius. 'But do not worry. We are merely passing by.'

It looked exactly like the ancient Coliseum they had seen up on the surface, but down here it was all there; nothing was missing. Every brick and slab of stone was in place. It looked as if it had been built very recently.

They walked on until they were in an alleyway leading down the side of the Coliseum.

Cassius stopped by a set of wooden doors and nodded at a sentry guarding the post. The sentry pulled open one of the doors.

'Good luck in there,' said Cassius, nudging Nick and Kat towards the door.

'B ... b ... but you said you were setting us free!' protested Nick, a horrible feeling bubbling in the pit of his stomach.

'I lied,' said Cassius. 'It's more exciting for the crowd if you are unprepared.'

He pushed them inside.

CHAPTER 7

Nick and Kat stumbled forward and stared around in horror as the door slammed shut behind them.

The Coliseum was huge. Rows and rows of spectators towered up towards the sky.

Huge candles and flaming torches were everywhere, throwing long shadows onto the ground. The floor of the arena was vast and covered in something that looked like sawdust.

As soon as the crowd spotted Nick and Kat, the shouting, whistling and cheering began.

'Are they pleased to see us, or are they excited about the prospect of us being killed by the beast?' asked Kat anxiously.

'I don't know,' replied Nick, 'but we'll need those.'

He pointed at two visors lying on the ground. Beside them were two shields and two swords, like the ones they had used earlier.

They put on the visors and grabbed the swords and shields.

'BRING ON THE BEAST! BRING ON THE BEAST!' chanted the crowd.

'Do you think it will be the same size as the model?' asked Kat, as they stood rooted to the spot, the crowd's noise getting louder by the second.

'I have no idea,' said Nick, 'but I'm pretty sure it will be terrifying.'

'BRING ON THE BEAST!' yelled the crowd. The noise was deafening.

'Look over there!' hissed Kat.

On the opposite side of the Coliseum two guards were slowly lifting a barred wooden gate.

'BRING ON THE BEAST! BRING ON THE BEAST!'

When the gate was fully open, for a few seconds nothing happened. Then one of the guards prodded something with a long stick. There was a terrifying roar and the beast stomped into the arena.

The crowd were on their feet, screaming and clapping and pumping their fists in the air.

Nick and Kat shrunk back in horror.

The beast was a million times scarier than the model they'd battled earlier.

Its eyes were a dark shade of blood-red, its oily green scales glinted in the torchlight and its claws and fangs were as long as Nick and Kat's arms.

The beast trotted around the side of the Coliseum for a few moments and sniffed the sawdust on the floor.

It looked at the crowd. Then it moved its vast head and saw Nick and Kat.

It shook its body, snorted loudly and charged.

CHAPTER 8

At incredible speed the beast raced across the Coliseum floor, kicking up clouds of sawdust in its wake.

It may have been very large, but it was very quick, too.

Its eyes were focused on Nick and Kat, its huge tongue was drooping out of its mouth, dripping saliva onto the ground.

Nick and Kat's hearts were racing like high-power speedboats. Their hands were clammy and sweat was running down their foreheads, under their visors and into their eyes.

'OK,' said Nick in a trembling voice. 'We know what we have to do.'

'You mean the diving thing?' asked Kat.

Nick nodded. 'Remember to hold your nerve,' he said.

On thundered the beast. The crowd loved it. Many were on their feet, cheering the beast on.

Suddenly, when it was less than a metre away, Nick dived to the left while Kat threw herself to the right.

They just managed to avoid the beast and, with no time to turn, it smashed its head against the wall.

It howled in pain – a spine-chilling roar that echoed round the whole Coliseum.

The crowd hissed and booed.

Nick and Kat were now sprinting at full speed. They were halfway to the other side of the arena when the beast straightened itself up and charged again.

'IT'S NEARLY ON US!' shouted Kat, looking over her shoulder in horror.

The beast thundered over the ground as it approached them. With a huge spring it leapt through the air to seize them.

But, with perfect timing, Nick and Kat threw themselves onto the floor and the beast flew over their bodies. It spun out of control and whacked its back against a pillar.

It screamed in agony.

Nick ran towards it and smashed it on the head as hard as he could with his shield. The beast roared with rage.

The crowd were angry now. They were hissing and jeering, and many people started throwing mouldy fruit and vegetables at Nick and Kat.

'That's helpful!' snarled Kat, kicking a rotten apple out of her way.

'Oh no!' shouted Nick. 'It's coming again!'

By now the beast was furious. Twice it had been cheated of its prey. It wasn't going to make a mistake the third time.

It had a look of steely determination in its eyes as it thundered towards them.

They sprinted in front of it and held up their swords.

But as they prepared to leap out of its way and then attack it, Nick tripped over a squashed potato skin and went crashing down onto the ground.

CHAPTER 9

Nick's sword and shield spun out of his hands and flew away across the Coliseum floor.

The crowd went crazy. At last, they were going to see something gruesome.

Nick struggled to get up.

'MOVE!' screamed Kat.

The beast was mere moments away from grabbing Nick when something large and round hit its back with a painful slap.

Kat had picked up a rotten melon off the floor and thrown it at the beast, like a cannon ball.

Screeching to a halt, the beast spun round and saw Kat, holding another melon and preparing to throw this one too.

The spectators were now on their feet – shrieking at the tops of their voices.

Nick grabbed his chance to stand up properly.

'There's an open door on the other side of the arena!' he shouted to Kat. 'Let's go for it.'

Kat nodded, chucked the melon she was holding – which hit the beast full in the face – and in a flash started racing across the arena.

She was joined a few seconds later by Nick. They had never run so fast.

The beast was angrier than ever and, with a great roar of fury, it stampeded after them, its claws making giant crunching sounds as it moved.

Nick and Kat were very near the open door now, with the beast a few metres behind them.

But as they approached the door it suddenly slammed shut in their faces.

'NOOO!' screamed Kat.

She and Nick stood with their backs up against the closed door.

Kat held her sword and shield up, but they both knew this would not be enough to stop the giant, roaring creature.

The beast pulled up and stood there, looming over them with an evil smile on its lips. Its sharp fangs glinted, the fur on its back stood up.

It took a few steps backwards and prepared to start its final, human-devouring charge.

Chapter 10

But before the beast took a step, Nick quickly pulled his mobile phone out of his trouser pocket, tapped on the screen and flung it in the beast's direction.

It landed at the beast's feet.

Earlier that day, Nick had been playing his favourite motorsport game and it was

still on PAUSE. Now, having pressed PLAY, Nick had restarted the game.

The beast looked down at the phone.

The pictures on the screen showed red, black and silver cars racing round a track.

The commentator's voice spilled out of the phone's speaker with music blaring underneath it. The digital lap times flashed.

It was all noise and colour and movement.

The beast made a strange throaty sound and stared at the phone.

'WHAT IS THAT EVIL THING?' shouted someone from the crowd.

'IS THIS DARK MAGIC?' screamed someone else.

The beast was fascinated by the phone. It ignored Nick, Kat and the crowd and crouched down on its haunches to study it more closely.

The crowd started booing and shouting furiously. They hadn't paid to see the beast sitting down.

Taking this as their cue to escape, Nick looked at Kat and pointed to the recently closed door.

Kat nodded and a few seconds later they were climbing up its wooden slats and then tumbling over the top.

As boos echoed around the Coliseum, Nick and Kat landed in a narrow alleyway.

At the end of the alleyway was a large, circular hole.

Beyond the hole they could see the street in front of the Coliseum, not an ancient Roman street but the modern street they'd been in a few hours ago.

Nick and Kat's hearts lifted with relief. It was obviously some kind of time hole.

Perhaps it was the only way they could get back to their own time. They needed to get through it!

But then, to their shock, the hole started closing.

In an instant they were running at full pelt, fists clenched, hearts beating wildly. The hole was closing quickly. In a few seconds it would be completely sealed up.

Nick and Kat kicked their heels and then launched themselves headfirst through the

air. First Kat and then Nick went flying through the hole.

As soon as they hit the pavement outside, the hole completely vanished.

'What on Earth are you two doing?'

It was their mum and dad. They were looking down at their children as if they'd just turned into aliens.

'Er … we were just play-fighting,' explained Kat breathlessly, standing up and brushing the dust of her clothes.

'Well forget that,' said their dad. 'There's a really interesting door on the other side of the road. I know how much you like exploring, Nick, so I say we go through it and see where it leads.'

Nick and Kat followed their father's gaze. He was pointing to the very same door that had led them into that tunnel – and a whole lot of trouble.

'Er … let's give that one a miss,' said Nick, getting to his feet.

'Really?' asked their dad.

'Yeah,' said Kat. 'There's probably something really beastly on the other side.'

Nick tried to hide a laugh.

'OK,' said their mum. 'Let's go inside the Coliseum.'

'Fine,' nodded Nick. 'But we'll only come if we can be spectators. We don't want to be fighters.'

Nick and Kat's parents gave their children another funny look before marching off, eager to see another incredible reminder of what ancient Rome had really looked like.

THE COLISEUM

The Coliseum in Rome is the largest amphitheatre in the world. It was built around 70AD and held around 50,000 to 80,000 people!

Gladiatorial games were held in the Coliseum. The Romans thought that the games made the gods happy and protected Rome from disaster.

GLADIATORS

There were about 30 different types of gladiator. They would fight against each other in battles to the death. Each type of gladiator had different armour, clothing and weapons.

Some gladiators fought large animals, usually lions or bears. Some fought on horseback. Others used a trident and a large net.

At the end of the battle, those who had been killed were dragged through the 'Gate of Death'. They would be stripped and their weapons and armour were given to the dead's gladiator master. The best gladiators could be granted freedom by the Emperor after a victory.

Now read the first chapter of another great
Toxic title by Jonny Zucker:

ISLAND SHOCK

CHAPTER 1

Mike Chen woke up with a start.

He opened his eyes slowly and had to hold up his hand to protect them from a glaring light.

The last thing he remembered was falling asleep at the airport terminal, where he'd been waiting to catch a plane.

He lowered his hand and was astonished by the sight that greeted him.

He was on a beach.

Sand stretched all around him. Gentle waters from a vast ocean lapped onto the shore. A couple of huge trees bearing strange orange fruit stood a short distance away on the sand.

There was no sign of Mac or Robbie, or any of the other kids from school who'd been waiting with him for the plane to France.

What on Earth was going on? Where was he – and how had he got here?

He scanned the ground for his rucksack. He couldn't see it.

Maybe Mr Masters had tricked them all, and instead of going to France he'd taken them to some remote island.

But if that was true, where were the others?

'MAC! ROBBIE! MR MASTERS!' he called.

Nothing. Just the sound of the sea.

Scratching his head in total bewilderment, Mike stood up and looked behind him.

A jungle of trees, bushes and wild grass lay before him, stretching into the distance as far as he could see.

It looked like he was on an island – one of those desert islands you sometimes see in the movies.

But it was impossible to tell from here how big the island was. It might be no more than a hundred metres. It might be thirty times that size.

Mike realised he was incredibly thirsty. He walked towards the trees and saw a small rock pool, fed by a tiny stream.

Crouching down, he cupped his hands and dipped them into the pool. Drinking from his hands, he was pleased to find that the water wasn't salty.

At least he had fresh water.

He had just splashed some water on his face when he heard a thumping sound a short way away.

He turned quickly to his right, but all he saw was the sea gently rolling up onto the beach.

But when he turned to his left his heart froze.

Snaking its way out of the jungle next to the sea, and whacking its tail on the ground, was a large, scaly, terrifying-looking crocodile.

MORE GREAT TOXIC READS

Action-packed adventure stories featuring jungles, swamps, deserted islands, robots, space travel, zombies, computer viruses and monsters from the deep.

How many have you read?

JONNY ZUCKER

THE BATTLE OF THE UNDERSEA KINGDOM

by Jonny Zucker

When the local mayor is kidnapped, the people suspect other villages of taking him. But Danny's dad, Tyler, knows more. He thinks that creatures from under the sea are to blame – and he's going to prove it!

MORE GREAT TOXIC READS

FOOTBALL FORCE

by Jonny Zucker

It's 2066 and football has changed. Players now wear lightweight body armour. Logan Smith wants to play for the best local team – Vestige United. Their players are fantastic, but Logan suspects that the team has a dark secret.

ISLAND SHOCK

by Jonny Zucker

Mike Chen wakes up on a deserted beach. The last thing he remembers is waiting for a flight at the airport. How did he get here? Where are his friends? Mike soon realises that he is surrounded by danger on all sides. Can he survive the attacks of wild creatures and find out what is going on?

MORE GREAT TOXIC READS

CRASH LAND EARTH

by Jonny Zucker

Jed and his friends are setting out on a trip to Mars. But their spaceship is in trouble and they are forced to crash-land back on Earth. But nothing is quite as it should be. Jed and his fellow explorers find themselves in a race against time to save planet Earth.

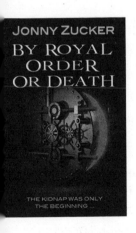

BY ROYAL ORDER OR DEATH

by Jonny Zucker

Miles is a member of the Royal Protection Hub, whose job is to protect the Royal family. When Princess Helena is kidnapped, Miles uncovers a cunning and dangerous plot. Miles must use all his skills to outwit the kidnappers and save the princess's life.

MORE GREAT TOXIC READS

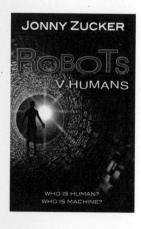

ROBOTS V HUMANS

by Jonny Zucker

Nico finds himself with five other kids – all his age. None of them can remember anything from their past. Then they are told that three of them are human and the other three are robots. Can Nico find out who is human and who are the robots?

ZOMBIE CAMP

by Jonny Zucker

Arjun and Kev are at summer camp. It's great – there's lots to do and places to explore. But after a while Arjun and Kev begin to suspect that nothing is quite as it seems. Can they avoid the terrible fate that awaits them?

MORE GREAT TOXIC READS

VIRUS 21

by Jonny Zucker

A new computer virus is rapidly spreading throughout the world. It is infecting everything, closing down hospitals, airports and even the internet. Can Troy and Macy find the hackers before the whole world shuts down?

TERROR OF THE SWAMP

by John Townsend

Ex-SAS explorer Baron and his son Greg have been sent to the African jungle to find a lost TV crew. It's a search that brings them face to face with the mysterious ancient terrors of the swamp – and it could cost them their lives.

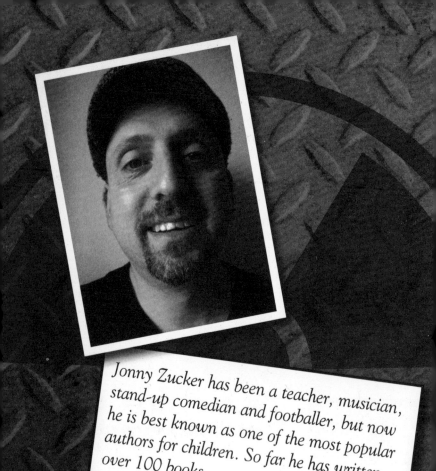

Jonny Zucker has been a teacher, musician, stand-up comedian and footballer, but now he is best known as one of the most popular authors for children. So far he has written over 100 books.

Jonny also plays in a band and has done over 60 gigs as a stand-up comedian, reaching the London Region Final of the BBC New Comedy awards.

He still dreams of being a professional footballer.